Mimi's Little Snowflakes

These look pretty hanging in a window!

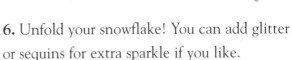

You'll need:

White paper, scissors

1. Cut out a circle of paper about the size you want your snowflake to be. It doesn't have to be perfectly round!

2. Fold the circle in half.

3. Then fold in half again and pinch the middle point to mark the center.

4. Open the paper up again. Then fold each side of the semicircle in, so that the center is now the point of a triangle.

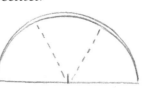

5. Carefully snip away shapes from each side of the triangle. Use the patterns shown here, or try your own. Just be sure to leave some uncut spots along each edge to hold the snowflake together.

6. Unfold your snowflake! You can add glitter or sequins for extra sparkle if you like.

Snowflake Pattern

Snowflake Pattern

This one makes heart shapes!

I love paper crafts!

'Twas two weeks before Christmas and all through the house,
not a creature was stirring, except Papa mouse. . . .

Christmas
with the
Mousekins

Maggie Smith

Alfred A. Knopf
New York

One bright winter morning, the whole Mousekin family bundled up and set off for Balsam Hill to find the perfect Christmas tree.

Yippee! Hooray! We get our tree today!

Hooray! Yippee! Today we get our tree!

"This one's too tall," said Papa.

"This one's too small," said Mama.

"This one's all wobbly," said Mimi.

"Look at this one!" Momo said.
"It's perfect!"
Everyone agreed.
So Papa cut it down, and they
took the tree home on the sled.

Later that very day, Nana Mousekin arrived for the holidays.
She was full of hugs for everyone, and her suitcase was full of surprises!

After warming up with some elderberry tea, Nana helped Mimi and Momo make some holiday decorations.

Mittens-in-a-Row

Mitten Pattern

You'll need:

Construction paper, scissors, ruler, tracing paper, pencil, glue, a penny, markers and glitter (optional)

To make mittens:

1. Cut a strip of paper 2 inches high and 11 inches long.

2. Fold the paper in half. Fold it in half again. Then fold it in half a third time!

3. Draw a mitten pattern on your paper. (You can draw it freehand, or you can trace the pattern on this page onto tracing paper, cut the pattern out, and then trace around it on your colored paper.)

4. Snip away the edges of the paper around the mitten pattern.

5. Unfold your mittens!

6. You can decorate your mittens with markers or glitter. Or you can make the snowflake decorations shown here.

To make a snowflake decoration:

1. Fold a narrow strip of paper in half two times so you have 4 layers.

2. Trace around a penny to make a circle.

3. Draw a line down the middle of the circle. Then draw an X, as shown.

4. Snip away little triangles between the pencil lines (don't cut into the middle!), and then cut around the edge of the circle. You should have 4 snowflakes!

5. Repeat these steps to make 4 more.

6. Glue snowflakes onto the mittens. Make more mittens-in-a-row and tape them together for a long garland!

Christmas-Trees-in-a-Row

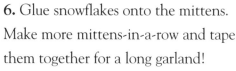

Tree Pattern

You can make a row of Christmas trees using the mitten instructions and this Christmas tree pattern. Attach the ends to make a circle of trees.

Momo's Christmas Tree Hat

Just like my hat!

You'll need:

Green poster board, 16 inches of elastic cording, pencil, ruler, scissors, glue, tape or stapler. To decorate, you could use: a pom-pom, ribbon, rickrack, paint, markers, glitter, sequins, buttons, beads, stickers!

To make the hat:

1. Make a semicircle of poster board:

a. Using a ruler, mark a spot 8 inches in from the corner.

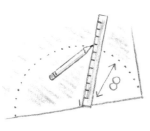

b. Then use that spot as the starting point and measure out 8 inches from it, making a series of dots in a fan shape.

c. Connect the dots to make a semicircle and cut it out.

2. Fold the semicircle in half and pinch the middle point to mark the center.

3. Open your semicircle up, and spread a line of glue along half the straight edge and a little way around the curve.

5 - 6"

4. Curl the paper around to form a cone, with the edges overlapping. The opening should be about 5 or 6 inches across. Press the glued edge in place and hold until set. Use some staples or tape to secure it even more.

5. Tie a knot at one end of your elastic cording. Place the cording just inside the hat, and staple or tape it below the knot.

6. Put the hat on your head and stretch the elastic around to measure the right length for you. Cut off the part you don't need.

7. Then tie a knot in the end and attach it to the opposite side of the hat.

To decorate the hat:

You can make your hat as simple or fancy as you like. Ribbon or yarn in a spiral looks nice. A pom-pom on top is fun!

While the grown-ups untangled and tested all the Christmas lights, Mimi and Momo wrote their letters to Santa.

Dear Santa Mouse,
How are you?
I am fine. (and still enjoying my gifts from last year!) This year I would love to get:
- A new paint set
- a pair of Polka dot boots.
Merry Christmas!
♡♡ from
Your friend,
Mimi Mousekin

dear Santa,
PLease bring me
A TeLLASKope,
A TRAK For my Karz
P.S. *** I HAV
bin good. * MOMO

Then everyone decorated the tree.

Ten days before Christmas, it was time for Momo's favorite activity: baking dozens of cookies to give away as gifts. (And making plenty to keep for themselves too!)

Gather, Measure, Mix, and Beat.
Let's Make Something Sweet to Eat.
Butter, Sugar, Flour, Spice.
Cinnamon Makes it TWICE as NICE!

Look—I making SNAILS!

Cinnamon Snails

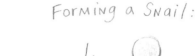
Forming a Snail:

1.

2.

3.

4. small coil for head — bigger coil for body

5.

Ingredients

4 tablespoons butter, softened
4 tablespoons cream cheese
½ cup brown sugar
1 egg
½ teaspoon vanilla extract
1½ cups flour
½ teaspoon baking powder

¼ teaspoon salt
¼ teaspoon cinnamon
cinnamon sugar:
  1 teaspoon cinnamon
  ¼ cup sugar
mini chocolate chips

I make the coils nice and tight.

BE SURE TO HAVE AN ADULT
HELP YOU IN THE KITCHEN.

To make the dough:

Preheat the oven to 375°.

Cream the butter, cream cheese, and brown sugar until light and fluffy. Add the egg and vanilla and mix until well blended. Combine the flour, baking powder, salt, and cinnamon and add gradually to form a soft dough.

To form the cookies:

Mix the cinnamon and sugar on a plate. Scoop out a rounded tablespoon of dough and roll it between floured hands to make a rope, about 6 inches long. Roll the rope in cinnamon sugar and then coil from both ends to make a snail shape. Place the cookies on parchment-lined cookie sheets, 2 inches apart. Bake for 10 minutes, or until the edges begin to brown. Cool on wire racks.

To decorate the cookies:

Press on mini chocolate chip eyes while the cookies are still warm from the oven.

Gingerbread Mice

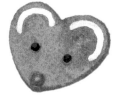

I dip the cookie cutter in flour so it won't stick to the dough.

Ingredients

3 cups all-purpose flour

¼ teaspoon salt

1 teaspoon baking soda

2 teaspoons ginger

1 teaspoon cinnamon

½ teaspoon nutmeg

¼ teaspoon allspice or cloves

12 tablespoons butter, softened

¾ cup brown sugar

½ cup molasses

1 egg

mini chocolate chips

cinnamon red hots (or dried
    cranberries or cherries)

royal icing: either store-bought
    white icing *or* whip 1 large egg
    white with 1⅓ cups powdered
    sugar until stiff glossy peaks form

To make the dough:

Whisk together the flour, salt, baking soda, and spices. In a large bowl,
cream the butter and the brown sugar until fluffy. Add the molasses
and the egg and beat well. Then gradually stir in the flour mixture.
Scrape the dough onto a sheet of plastic wrap, flatten it into a disk,
wrap tightly, and refrigerate for at least 2 hours.

To form the cookies:

Preheat the oven to 350°.

On a floured surface, roll out the dough to about
⅛ inch thick and cut out with a heart-shaped
cookie cutter. Transfer the hearts to greased cookie
sheets, leaving an inch between cookies. Bake 8 to
10 minutes for small hearts, 10 to 12 minutes for
larger ones. (For softer, chewier cookies, roll the
dough to about ¼ inch thick and bake for the
shorter amount of time.) Cool the cookies on the
sheets for a minute and then transfer to wire racks
to cool completely.

To decorate the cookies:

To make mouse faces, press on chocolate chip eyes
while the cookies are still warm from the oven.
When the cookies have cooled, pipe ears with royal
icing. Attach a cinnamon red hot (or a bit of dried
cranberry or cherry) with icing for the nose.

A week before Christmas, a fresh snowfall brought everyone outside.

I keep my ankles
stiff and straight;
I skate, I skate
a figure eight!

I push, then
WHOOSH—
I start to fly!
Just me, my sled,
the snow and sky.

Snowmouse, Snowmouse, pure and white,
how you make the season bright.
Mismatched mittens, ears askew—
Snowmouse, Snowmouse, we love you!

DECK the halls with pears and cherries!
Fa la la la la, la la la la.
STRING the popcorn and cranBERRies!
Fa la la la la, la la la la.
VisitING with friends and MOUSEkins!
Fa la la, fa la la, la la la.
SINGing songs of celeBRAtion!
Fa la la la la, la la la la.

Five days before Christmas, carolers traveled from house to house,
filling the neighborhood with the jubilant sounds of the season.

The Mousekins welcomed them
with hot drinks and tasty treats.

Peppermint Cocoa
Make your favorite kind of cocoa, and
add two peppermint candies or
stir it with a peppermint stick
or candy cane.

'Twas the day before Christmas and all through the house, all the Mousekins were busy (except Baby mouse). With so little time left and so much to do, they were finishing presents and wrapping them too.

I'll never finish everything in time!

Where are my scissors?

Finally all the presents had been wrapped and put under the tree. The stockings were hung, and a big plate of cookies and cheese was set out for Santa Mouse. Now it was time for Nana Mousekin's Christmas Eve Story.

"A long, long time ago," she began, "when your father was just a teeny-tiny baby—can you imagine that?"

"NO!" said Mimi and Momo, for although they heard the same story every year, they still could not believe that Papa mouse had ever been a little baby!

"Well," Nana continued, "it was two days before Christmas, and we were nearly out of sugar, milk, and cheese. So your grandpa set off for the store, which was two whole hours away, and he promised to be back for supper.

"But a few hours later, big scary clouds swept in from the west on howling winds. Then the snow started to fall—huge thick snowflakes, as big as teacups! Before long, the whole world was coated, and I could only see white out the window.

"I put the baby to bed and tried to stay calm, but I was worried sick about Grandpa. Was he lost in the storm? Would he freeze to death far from home? If he did make his way back, would he find the house, so buried in snow? How would he even get inside?

"All night I sat fretting by the fire, but I must have dozed off because suddenly I was startled awake by a loud thump on the roof. 'The house is falling in!' I screamed as great heaps of snow fell down the chimney. But right then, there was a second great thump, and guess who landed in the fireplace?"

"Grandpa Mousekin!" said Momo.

"That's right," said Nana. "And guess who followed right behind him?"

"Santa Mouse!" said Mimi.

"He had rescued your grandpa from the storm and delivered him home, supplies and all, safe and sound!"

"Wow!" exclaimed Momo. "What did he look like?"

"His eyes," Nana remembered, "how they twinkled! His dimples, how merry!

His cheeks were like roses, his nose like a cherry. He had a broad face and a little round belly that shook when he laughed—like a bowl full of jelly!"

"Did you offer him something to eat?" asked Mama mouse.

"Of course! I put out a plate of my special pinwheel cookies," said Nana, "and he munched down two right away. 'Delicious!' he declared, brushing crumbs from his coat. 'But if it's not too much trouble . . .' And he asked for something else to go with them."

"Cheese!" said Momo.

"That's right," said Papa. "That's how we know that Santa Mouse likes a little cheese with his cookies."

"He didn't stay long," Nana concluded, "because he had so much to do. He knew the storm would slow things down—that's why he had started a day early, and that was very lucky for us, wasn't it? He went back up the chimney, and got into his sleigh, and we heard him exclaim as he drove out of sight: *'Happy Christmas to all, and to all a good night!'*"

PRESENTS

I love presents, yes I do—
one for me and one for you.
Shiny wrappings, silver bows,
day by day the pile grows.
Ears are tuned and eyes are wide—
busy guessing: What's inside?
(Papa thinks it's socks or ties;
he's in for a big surprise!)
Tall ones, small ones, flat ones—look—
a box of chocolates, or a book?
One for Brother, Baby too—
this one says "From You Know Who."
It's awfully big—what could it be?
I'm so excited—it's for me!

Baby Mouse's Christmas Mobile

For all the crafts on these pages, you'll need: tracing paper, sharp pencil, ruler, fabric scissors, glue, straight pins (optional).

You'll need:

Red, green, and yellow felt, heavy thread (or embroidery floss)

1. Trace the patterns on this page onto tracing paper and cut out.

2. Carefully trace (or pin) your patterns onto felt and cut out 2 green trees, 2 yellow stars, 4 red hearts, 4 yellow hearts, and 8 red dots.

3. Cut three lengths of thread or embroidery floss: one 10 inches long, one 5 inches, and one 3 inches.

4. Spread glue on one red heart.

5. Lay one end of the 3-inch thread in the middle of the heart, as shown, then top with another red heart and press down. Let dry for 5 minutes.

6. Repeat steps 4–5 with your remaining red hearts, using the 5-inch length of thread.

7. Glue the yellow hearts onto both sides of the red hearts and let dry.

8. Spread glue on one tree and one star.

9. Position your star ½ inch above the tree, and lay the 10-inch thread over both the tree and the star, as shown.

10. Next lay the tops of the threads from your hearts at the bottom of the tree, as shown.

11. Now place the second green tree and yellow star on top of their mates, press down, and let dry.

12. Glue the small red circle ornaments onto your tree.

13. Fold over the top thread and make a knot to form a hanging loop for your mobile.

Cut 4 red hearts

Cut 4 yellow hearts

Cut 2 green trees

Cut 8 red dots

Cut 2 yellow stars

Momo's Mousie Sock Puppet

You'll need:

Pink and black felt, heavy white thread (or string or dental floss), one child's sock—pale blue is pretty!

1. Trace the patterns on this page onto tracing paper and cut out.

2. Carefully trace (or pin) your patterns onto felt and cut out 2 pink ears, 1 pink nose, 1 pink tail, and 2 black eyes.

3. Lay your sock flat with the heel side up.

4. Position the ears about 1 inch from the toe, as shown.

5. Glue the ears on, spreading glue in the shaded areas only. Press down and let dry.

6. Cut 3 pieces of thread, each 5 inches long. Gather the pieces of thread together and tie a knot in the center.

7. Glue the whiskers on the sock's toe, and glue the nose on top of the whiskers' center knot. Press down to set.

8. Glue on eyes and let dry about 5 minutes.

9. Glue the tail inside the cuff of the sock, as shown, and let dry.

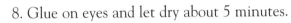

Cut 2 pink ears

Cut 1 pink tail

Cut 1 pink nose

Cut 2 black eyes

Mimi's Mitten Bookmark

You'll need:

Red and white felt, embroidery floss, yarn or narrow ribbon

1. Trace the patterns on this page onto tracing paper and cut out.

2. Carefully trace (or pin) your patterns onto felt and cut out 4 red mittens, 20 white triangles, and 4 wavy white strips.

3. Cut a length of embroidery floss 12 inches long.

4. Place two mittens side by side and spread glue on them. Lay about 1 inch of each end of the embroidery floss on the mittens, as shown.

5. Position the remaining mittens on top, press down, and let dry for 5 minutes.

6. Glue 5 white triangles on each side of each mitten to make a flower pattern, as shown, and glue wavy strips on the mittens' wrists. Let dry.

Cut 4 mittens

Cut 4 wavy strips

Cut 2 white strips, then cut into triangles

Later, after a splendid Christmas feast of three-cheese soufflé, winter squash soup supreme, and gingerbread upside-down cake, the Mousekins delivered cookies to all their friends and neighbors.

Next year, Let's make something special for them!

"What a glorious Christmas we've had," said Mama.
And everyone agreed.

Christmas Magic
Silver Lights
Hush of Secrets
Starry Nights
Bright Traditions
Old and New
Mem'ries Kept
The Whole Year
Through

'Twas the day after Christmas and all through the house,
not a creature was stirring, except Mimi mouse.
She was writing a thank-you for all the good cheer
that Santa Mouse brought to her family this year. . . .

To my wonderful editor,
Nancy Siscoe,
whose heavenly holiday confections
always make Christmas
Even Merrier!

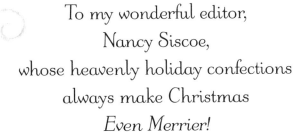

Many, many mouse-hugs to Sarah Hokanson
for her infinite inspiration (and patience) with this book! xoxo

THIS IS A BORZOI BOOK PUBLISHED BY ALFRED A. KNOPF

Copyright © 2010 by Maggie Smith

All rights reserved. Published in the United States by Alfred A. Knopf, an imprint of Random House Children's Books,
a division of Random House, Inc., New York.

Knopf, Borzoi Books, and the colophon are registered trademarks of Random House, Inc.

Visit us on the Web! www.randomhouse.com/kids

Educators and librarians, for a variety of teaching tools, visit us at www.randomhouse.com/teachers

Library of Congress Cataloging-in-Publication Data

Smith, Maggie.

Christmas with the Mousekins / Maggie Smith.

p.   cm.

Summary: A mouse family tells stories, bakes cookies, makes crafts, and more as they prepare for Christmas. Includes directions for each of the crafts and recipes for cookies.

ISBN 978-0-375-83330-4 (trade) — ISBN 978-0-375-93330-1 (lib. bdg.)

[1. Christmas—Fiction. 2. Mice—Fiction. 3. Family life—Fiction.] I. Title.

PZ7.S65474Chr 2010

[E]—dc22

2010003878

The illustrations in this book were created using watercolors, gouache, and acrylic paints on watercolor paper.

MANUFACTURED IN CHINA

September 2010

10 9 8 7 6 5 4 3 2 1   First Edition

Angel-Mouse Tree-topper

You'll need:

Pretty wrapping paper; 2 sheets of 8½-x-11-inch white card stock; 4-inch square of yellow or gold card stock; scraps of pink, red, and black card stock; 3-inch length of paper-towel tube; tracing paper; sharp pencil; glue; scissors; ruler; paper clips; pink pencil or crayon; gold or metallic marker (optional)

1. To make your pretty wrapping paper sturdy for the dress: Cover a sheet of white card stock with a thin layer of glue. Lay wrapping paper on top and press down, smoothing out any creases. Stack some books on top until the glue dries.

2. On the back of the reinforced wrapping paper, measure a 5½-inch semicircle, as shown, and cut out.

3. Fold the semicircle in half and pinch to mark the center point, then unfold. Spread glue along the edge, as shown, then curl the paper around to make a cone, overlapping the ends about 2 inches. Use paper clips to secure or hold until set.

4. Trace all the patterns here onto tracing paper and cut out.

5. For the arms, fold the remaining reinforced wrapping paper in half. Place the pattern flush with the folded edge, as shown, trace, and cut out.

6. For the wings, fold a sheet of white card stock in half. Place the pattern on the fold, as shown, trace, and cut out.

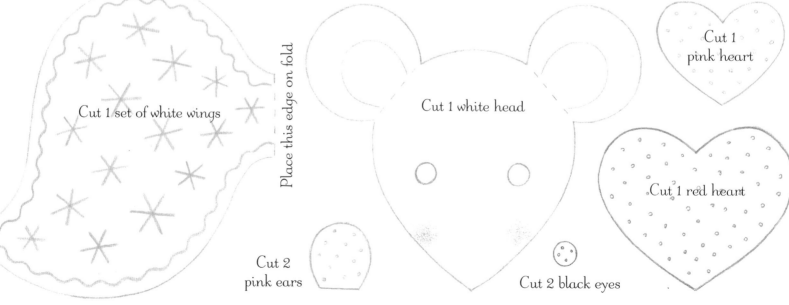

Cut 1 set of white wings

Place this edge on fold

Cut 1 white head

Cut 1 pink heart

Cut 1 red heart

Cut 2 pink ears

Cut 2 black eyes